P9-DGH-271

YEARLING BOOKS are designed especially to entertain and enlighten young people. Charles F. Reasoner, Professor Emeritus of Children's Literature and Reading, New York University, is consultant to this series.

For a complete listing of all Yearling titles, write to Dell Publishing Co., Inc., Promotion Department, P.O. Box 3000, Pine Brook, N.J. 07058.

Jeeter,
Mason and
the
Magic Headset

by Maggie Twohill

A YEARLING BOOK

Published by
Dell Publishing Co., Inc.
1 Dag Hammarskjold Plaza
New York, New York 10017

Yearling ® TM 913705, Dell Publishing Co., Inc.

ISBN: 0-440-44220-6

Reprinted by arrangement with Bradbury Press, An Affiliate of Macmillan, Inc.

Printed in the United States of America

December 1986

10 9 8 7 6 5 4 3 2 1

CW

This is for
Caity and Braden LuBell

Contents

ONE

Sisters

"You are my ba-by,
Yeah, you are my ba-bee,
Yeah, yeah, yeah, yeah —"

"Jeeter, turn that radio down!" Carol-Ann hollered from the kitchen.

"—bay-yay-yay-yay-BEE—"

"Jeeter! Turn that *down!*"

Jeeter Huff rolled over on the living room rug and turned the dial on the stereo-radio set almost all the way to the left. She thought she'd heard a noise. She frowned and listened very carefully, craning her neck forward. Nothing. Silence. Jeeter shrugged and reached for the dial again.

"Yeah-yeah-yeah-yeah, ba-bee—"

"JEETER!"

Jeeter sat up quickly, and this time she turned the music completely off. The vibrations in the floor stopped.

"Did someone say something?" Jeeter called.

Carol-Ann Huff, Jeeter's thirteen-year-old sister, stomped into the living room.

"*I* said something." Carol-Ann spoke through clenched teeth. "I said something about twelve times. I can't study when you play that radio so loud. I can't even *think*, Jeeter. I used to like that rock station until you started blasting us all out of the house!"

Jeeter looked around from her position on the floor.

"Where are Mom and Dad?" she asked.

"I just told you. You blasted them out of the house!"

"I *did*?"

Carol-Ann knelt down next to her sister. "They told you on their way out. They were going down the street to look at the Johnsons' slides of Bermuda.

I'm supposed to baby-sit for you. They told you."

"They did?" Jeeter wrinkled her nose. "Well . . . I guess they did. I mean, I saw them moving their lips as they went out the door . . ."

"You can't hear anything above that music and neither can anyone else."

Jeeter grinned. "But that's the way I like it. I like to feel the beat, right through the floor!"

Carol-Ann sighed. "Jeeter—You're not even a teenager yet. You're not even *ten* yet. You should still be listening to—to Mother Goose rhymes or something. Leave the rock to the big kids." She stood up.

"I like it," Jeeter said. "I like the music. I like the groups. I *like* it, Carol-Ann."

"So like it. But like it softer!" Carol-Ann stalked back into the kitchen.

Jeeter made a pouty face. She reached for the dial again and turned it slightly to the right. The sound could barely be heard, but Jeeter recognized it. It was the latest single by one of her favorite groups—The Elephant Herd. She forgot about Carol-Ann. She bit on her lower lip and began to smile.

"Oh, yeah . . . All right . . ."

Jeeter's smile widened. She brought her forefinger close to the radio dial and flicked it. A bit. Just a tiny bit to the right.

> *"We're goin' out to-night!*
> *Oh, yeah . . . All right . . . "*

A little more. Just a litte louder. A teensy-weensy bit louder.

"WE'RE GOIN' OUT TO—NI-YI-YI-YIGHT"

Carol-Ann was in the room before Jeeter could blink. She reached behind the floor lamp and pulled the radio's plug out of its socket. The room was suddenly silent except for Carol-Ann's breathing. Jeeter rolled into a ball on the rug and covered her head.

Carol-Ann glared at the ball. "I'm not going to hit you," she said.

Jeeter didn't move.

"But I want to!"

"I only meant to turn it up a little," Jeeter said. "My finger slipped."

"You're going to bed," Carol-Ann said. "Come on. Get up and go upstairs."

"But it's only seven-thirty," Jeeter wailed.

"Too bad. I'm in charge now. And I say you're going to bed."

"But it's the night before my birthday!" Jeeter cried. "Are you going to punish me on the night before my tenth birthday?"

Carol-Ann looked down at her. " 'Night befores' don't count. And besides"—she grinned—"no matter how you look at it, you'll still be ten and I'll be thirteen and a half, so I can still tell you what to do."

Jeeter opened her eyes and peeked through her fingers at her sister.

"Come *on*, Jeeter. I have a big math test tomorrow and you ruined a whole half-hour of studying for me. So get upstairs!"

Slowly, Jeeter got to her feet, being sure to keep as much distance as she could between herself and Carol-Ann. When she reached the stairs, she broke away and began to run, calling over her shoulder, "Ha-ha, I'll just turn on the radio in Mom and Dad's room!"

Carol-Ann charged for her, muttering, "Oh, no, you don't!" as both of them pushed and jostled each other in their race upstairs.

Jeeter bolted for her parents' room, but Carol-Ann grabbed her by the waist and pulled her back, with Jeeter squealing and giggling.

"*Your* room, Jeeter," Carol-Ann said, holding on to her.

"Okay, okay!" Jeeter cried and Carol-Ann let go.

". . . *If* you tell me what I'm getting for my birth-day."

"No!"

"Is it a Cabbage Patch Kid? Is it, Carol-Ann, is it? Am I getting a Cabbage Patch Kid?"

"I'm not telling. You better get into your room, Jeeter . . ."

"Won't go till you tell me," Jeeter sang with her eyes sparkling.

Carol-Ann leaned forward toward her. "O-*kay*," she said.

"Huh?"

"I said okay. I'll *tell* you what you're getting for your birthday. I'll just tell you everything and spoil the whole surprise!"

"No," Jeeter said.

"Yes!" Carol-Ann cried. "One of the things is—"

"I'm shutting my ears!" Jeeter cried, covering her ears with her hands and running for her room. "I can't hear! I can't hear!" She kicked the door closed with her foot, but kept her hands over her ears until she was sure that Carol-Ann had gone back down-stairs, having gotten her own way.

Jeeter walked over to her bed and looked at her worn collection of dolls and stuffed animals.

"I don't even wish I was thirteen," Jeeter said to them. "Because then Carol-Ann would be sixteen, and she'd be even better at getting me to do what she wants!"

She flopped down on her bed.

"Oh, well," she said, picking up a teddy bear with one ear torn off. "At least I'll be ten tomorrow and that's better than nine." She hugged the bear. "I really didn't want Carol-Ann to tell me," she said in his one ear, "but I hope I do get a Cabbage Patch Kid, I really hope I do." She looked over the bear's shoulder at the other dolls. "But don't get the idea it'll take the place of any of you," she promised them. "I'll still love you all just the same. Just like any mama would."

Wishes

Jeeter sat on the living room floor with her birthday presents arranged in front of her. The boxes were all of different shapes and had different colored wrappings and ribbons. Jeeter stared at the pile with shining eyes.

"Here, Jeeter," her mother said. "Open this one." She smiled at Jeeter's father as she touched a large oblong box.

"Yeah, open that one, Jeet," Mr. Huff said. "I've been waiting all week for this special event."

"Me, too," Jeeter said, tearing the paper off the box. "Ah," she breathed when she saw what was inside.

"Let's see!" her friend Claudia Sykes said, peering over Jeeter's shoulder. Claudia was the only friend Jeeter had decided to invite to her family party. She had known Claudia since they'd been in nursery school together. "Oh!" Claudia cried. "It's a Cabbage Patch Kid! I have one, too!"

"But not like this one!" Jeeter held up the doll. "They're all different. Look, Claudia, look, Carol-Ann—it's a newborn *baby*. It has no hair yet. And look at the dimples."

"It's cute," Carol-Ann acknowledged. "What's the name on the birth certificate?"

Jeeter reached into the box and pulled out the papers that had come with the doll. "Um . . . His name is Oliver Harvey."

"That's nice," Claudia said. "Mine is Tracy Regina."

"I'm not keeping that name," Jeeter said, hugging the doll.

"You have to keep the name, silly," Claudia told her. "That's the whole idea. It comes with a birth certificate and adoption papers and a *name*, Jeeter!"

"But I didn't get to pick the name," Jeeter said. "And since I'm his mother, I pick his name. His name is . . . Mason."

"Mason what?"

"Mason *Huff*," Jeeter said.

"Open *my* present now, Jeeter!" Carol-Ann said.

"What is it?" Jeeter asked.

"Do you think I'd tell you?" Carol-Ann smirked. "And spoil the surprise?"

And Jeeter really *was* surprised!

Jeeter lay on her bed. It was still her birthday and would be until midnight and she wanted to enjoy every last bit of it. She was ten years old. She would be writing two numbers for her age from now on instead of one. And her party had been terrific. Mom and Dad had prepared her favorite supper: hot dogs and macaroni-and-cheese. Carol-Ann had baked the birthday cake: chocolate with pink frosting and butter-cream roses. Jeeter had been kept out of the kitchen until everything was ready, which was fine with her because she and Claudia played "guess what's in all the boxes" until it was time to eat.

And her presents were wonderful! Jeeter had to smile to herself in the dark. She couldn't have asked for better presents. Mason, her very own Cabbage Patch Kid. And the cute straw hat from Claudia. But Carol-Ann's present astonished her. She'd never expected anything like it!

She put Carol-Ann's present on, picked up Mason and tiptoed down the hall in the dark to her sister's room.

She rapped softly on the door.

"Carol-Ann? You up?"

"Yes . . ." Carol-Ann whispered hoarsely. "What's the matter?"

Jeeter pushed open the door. She could see Carol-Ann in the moonlight, curled up in her bed.

"It's late, Jeeter. How come you're not asleep?"

"I was too excited. I love my presents so much—and yours is so terrific—I just wanted to say thank you again!"

Carol-Ann sat up. "Well . . ." she said, "Dad and Mom really bought the radio. I only bought the headset. I see you're wearing it . . ."

"I know! I love it! See? The radio's clipped to my pajamas . . ." Jeeter clicked the radio on at her waist.

Carol-Ann clicked her tongue. "I'm glad you like it," she said.

Jeeter said, "What?"

"I said, 'I'm glad you like it'!" Carol-Ann repeated.

"I can't hear you . . ." Jeeter took off the headset and placed it over her doll's ears. "Here, Mason," she said, "you listen for a while. What did you say, Carol-Ann?"

"Never mind . . ."

"It's so neat, isn't it?" Jeeter bubbled. "I can carry my music around with me instead of having to use the big stereo in the living room. And nobody has to hear any of the sound except me!"

Carol-Ann leaned back against her pillow. "I *know*, Jeeter," she said. "That was the whole *idea!*"

"Well . . . but thanks, Carol-Ann."

Carol-Ann smiled. "You're a pain sometimes," she said, "but sometimes you're not. Happy birthday, kid."

"Thanks. Want to hear what I wished for when I blew out the candles?"

"No."

"Sure you do," Jeeter said.

"I don't. I don't care."

"Okay, then."

Carol-Ann sighed. "Oh, all right. What did you wish for?"

"Never mind."

"Jeeter . . ."

"Never mind, forget it. It was dumb."

"So what was it?"

"I mean it. It was dumb. Everyone was rushing me to blow out the candles before the wax dripped on the frosting and I didn't know what to wish for because I already got everything I wished for when I opened my presents, so I—"

"Jeeter! *What was it?*" Carol-Ann whispered as loud as she could without waking their parents.

"It was so dumb! I just wished I had a fairy godmother. I couldn't think of anything else to say."

Carol-Ann sat back. "That was dumb, Jeet," she said.

"I told you."

"G'night, Jeet," Carol-Ann said.

" 'Night." Jeeter headed for the door, carrying Mason. The doll was still wearing the headset.

"Oh, Jeeter?"

"What?"

"You know the two blouses Aunt Betty and Uncle Steve sent you?"

"Yeah . . ."

"Do you think the blue one just might possibly fit me . . . or would it really be too small?"

Who's Afraid of a Headset?

The day after Jeeter's birthday was a Saturday, a beautiful spring day. Jeeter couldn't wait to get out in it, even if she had been up late the night before, talking to Carol-Ann and then playing her radio until she finally fell asleep.

She bounced out of bed, remembered to brush her teeth but not her hair and clipped the new radio to her jeans. She removed her headset from Mason's ears, plugged it into the radio and put it on.

"Thanks for holding it for me, Mason," she said to the doll. She turned on the radio. Then, snapping her fingers, Jeeter hopped down the stairs to the beat of Station W-HIZ.

She saw her mother's lips move as she entered the kitchen, but Jeeter was listening hard to her music, so she just kept snapping and bopping.

As her mother reached for a bottle of vitamin pills, Jeeter saw her lips move again. Her mother was making faces at her. Angry faces. Jeeter whipped off the headset.

"Sorry, Mom. What did you say?"

"I said '*good morning*'!" Mrs. Huff yelled.

"Then how come you're so mad if it's such a good morning?" Jeeter wanted to know.

Her mother sighed. "Here's your vitamin and here's your grapefruit juice, and Jeeter Huff, you cannot simply cut yourself off from the world that way."

"What way?"

"When you're wearing those earphones, you don't hear anything else. That's not only annoying for people trying to talk to you, it's also dangerous. You could be hurt. You could be run over."

Jeeter drank the juices and wiped her mouth with the rim of the glass.

"I'll be careful," she said.

"You'd better be. And brush your hair!"

After breakfast, Jeeter plunked Claudia's straw hat over her headset and got ready to get her skateboard from the garage. "Would you like to come, Mason?" she asked. The doll was sitting up on the bed between the one-eared teddy and a China doll named Anna May Wong. "The other dolls all know the neighborhood, but you don't . . ."

Mason stared straight ahead, his puffy cheeks making his mouth seem smaller.

"I guess maybe you'd better take a nap," Jeeter said. "I'll be going pretty fast on my skateboard and it might be scary for you."

She went outside and soon was whizzing down the sidewalk, snapping her fingers. She felt wonderful! She decided to skate over to her school. The night before, Claudia had said there would be lots of kids using the playground if the weather was nice.

Big Beaver Elementary School was just three blocks from Jeeter's house. It had a large playground area on one side for the younger children and an even larger field in back where the older ones played soccer and baseball. There was also a basketball court at one end of the field.

The school grounds were crowded with kids. Jeeter recognized a group of girls from her class skipping rope. She was about to skate over to them when something touched her shoulder. Jeeter jumped and quickly took off her headset.

"Good morning, Jeeter."

Jeeter looked around and saw her teacher, Mrs. Bonino.

"G'morning, Mrs. Bonino . . ."

"I guess you didn't hear me with those headphones on," the teacher said.

Jeeter grinned. "I got them for my birthday. From my sister. What are you doing here, Mrs. Bonino? It's Saturday!"

"Well, I have some work to do. And I thought I'd have some peace and quiet. But the playground's so crowded! What are *you* doing here, Jeeter?"

"Well . . ." Jeeter grinned. "I have some playing to do."

Mrs. Bonino smiled. "Have a nice day, then. And happy birthday, Jeeter."

Jeeter said, "Thank you!", put her headset back on and skated over toward her friends. She could see Claudia turning one end of the rope. She waved.

The girls yelled something at her.

"What?"

They yelled again.

"What?"

"Take off your headset!" Claudia cried and pointed at her ears.

"I better take off my headset," Jeeter said.

"Did you get that radio and phones for your birthday?" Patsy McDonald asked.

"Uh-huh. Want to listen?"

"Okay . . ."

Jeeter handed Patsy the headset and turned up the radio.

"Ow, Jeeter!" Patsy cried. "Too loud!"

"Sorry! I wanted to make sure you'd hear it."

"I'll never hear anything again," Patsy said, rubbing her ears. "Here, take it back. What else did you get?"

"She got that cute straw hat from me," Claudia said. "I just love it."

"And what else?"

"A Cabbage Patch Kid . . ."

"I got one for Christmas," Susan Babcock said. "A little girl with yellow braids."

"Mine's a baby boy," Jeeter said, "and he's bald. I also got a bathing suit—"

"What color?"

"Red and white," Claudia answered for her.

"And what else?" Cathy Morgan asked.

"Tell us afterward," Susan said. "It's my turn to jump. You want to play, Jeeter? Last-in has to turn, though . . ."

"Okay!" Jeeter put her headset back on and took one end of the rope.

The girls started the chorus of an old, well-known skip-rope chant as Susan jumped.

"A my name is Alice and my husband's name is Al! We come from Al-a-ba-ma and we sell apples! B my name is Barbara and—"

But Jeeter was listening to a group called The Rebels on her radio, and they were singing something else. Jeeter's arm automatically began to turn in rhythm to The Rebels' song and not to the skip-rope chant. Susan tripped and fell in a tangled length of clothesline.

"*Jee*-ter!" Five girls looked angrily at her.

"I'm sorry . . . I didn't mean to!"

"I scraped my knee," Susan wailed.

"Gee, Susan—"

"Listen, Jeeter," Claudia said, "either you play with us or you listen to your radio. You can't do both."

Jeeter made a face. "Oh, boy," she said softly.

"Make up your mind," Patsy said.

Jeeter stood, still holding her end of the rope, trying to decide.

"Come *on*, Jeeter—"

"Oh, okay . . ." She unclipped the radio from her waist and put it and the headset on the grass next to her skateboard.

"Good," Claudia said. "Susan, you can have another turn."

"You can have *my* turn," Jeeter offered. "I'll skip a turn."

Susan clicked her tongue. It was hard to stay mad at Jeeter. "All right," she said, rubbing her sore knee. "I just hope I can still jump . . ."

Jeeter turned and jumped and chanted for a while, but her heart wasn't in it. She kept sneaking glances toward her radio. When Gloria Woolsey missed on "F my name is Florence," Jeeter decided to stop.

"I'm hungry," she said. "I guess I'll go home now."

"But it's not even lunch time," Claudia said.

"I know. But I'm hungry, anyway. Maybe I'll see you later."

Cathy Morgan made a face. "*I* think you just want to listen to that radio, Jeeter," she said.

"But that's so boring!" Claudia cried, waving her arms. "I mean, it's okay while you're doing your homework or something, but when you could be *playing*—?"

"I'm not allowed to listen to the radio when I'm doing my homework," Susan said.

Claudia said, "I listen all the time."

"And you flunk all the time," Susan said, laughing. Claudia glared at her.

Jeeter clipped on her radio, put on her headset and hat, tucked her skateboard under her arm and waved goodbye to her friends.

After lunch the sky began to darken and soon it was raining. Jeeter didn't mind. She lay on the living room floor with her headset over her ears, hugging

Mason and tapping her feet, while her father watched a ball game being rained out and her mother read the Saturday paper. Carol-Ann's friend Lulu came over to the Huffs', and after Lulu had shouted "Hi!" at Jeeter three times and got no answer, Carol-Ann marched up to her sister and pulled off the headset.

"Look at that!" Carol-Ann cried to an astonished Jeeter. "They come off!"

"Huh?" Jeeter said.

"I thought your head sprouted wires when you turned ten and that they were on for life!"

"You were the one who gave them to me," Jeeter said and reached for the headset Carol-Ann was holding high in the air above her.

"Yeah, and now I don't know if I'm glad or sorry," Carol-Ann said, still holding the headset out of Jeeter's reach.

"Give 'em to me," Jeeter whined.

"Now, girls," Mrs. Huff said. "Stop that right now. Jeeter, ever since lunch you've done nothing but wiggle around the floor snapping your fingers. I wish you'd find something else to do."

Carol-Ann made a smug face at Jeeter.

"Carol-Ann," her mother went on, "why don't you and Lulu take Jeeter with you up to your room. I don't want her buried inside that radio any more today."

Carol-Ann's expression changed instantly. "But Mo-om," she wailed. "She's ten!"

Mrs. Huff looked up.

"I mean, she's only *ten!*" Carol-Ann repeated. "Lulu and I have . . . *things* to discuss."

"Oh," her mother sighed. "Thirteen year olds have *things* to discuss."

"That's right," Carol-Ann said.

Mr. Huff looked up from the TV, where stadium workers were spreading a tarpaulin over the infield.

"Carol-Ann, you heard your mother. Take Jeeter up to your room, please. It won't hurt you to spend some time with your sister."

"It most certainly *will*," Carol-Ann snorted, but she allowed Jeeter to trail behind her up the stairs, her headset resting around her neck.

Lulu and Carol-Ann sat on Carol-Ann's bed and Jeeter plunked herself onto the floor.

"Okay, go ahead," Jeeter said.

"Go ahead *what?*"

"Go ahead and discuss your *things.*"

"Oh," Carol-Ann said in disgust.

"I won't interrupt," Jeeter said. "Go ahead."

Lulu and Carol-Ann looked at each other.

"Listen," Lulu said finally, "I was talking to you-know-who yesterday afternoon and—"

"Who?" Carol-Ann said.

"*You* know . . . R.G."

"Who's R.G.?" Jeeter asked, but they ignored her.

"Really?" Carol-Ann said.

"Uh-huh. And you-know-*who* said that you-know-who-*else* was going you-know-*where* this weekend. With you-know-who!"

"They *were*?" Carol-Ann shrieked.

"Who?" Jeeter asked. "Where?"

"Yes!" Lulu cried, ignoring Jeeter again, and she and Carol-Ann began to giggle.

Jeeter crossed her legs and propped her chin on her hands.

"And did you hear about E.F.?" Carol-Ann asked.

"What *I* heard may not be the same as what *you* heard. What did *you* hear?"

"Well!" Carol-Ann leaned over and whispered something behind her hand. Lulu laughed and clapped.

"*I* . . . didn't hear *anything*," Jeeter sighed.

"And *then*," Lulu said, and she leaned toward Carol-Ann and whispered something else.

"What?" Jeeter asked. "What's so funny? Who's going where? And why?"

"Oh, Jeeter," Carol-Ann said, "just go sit over there and listen to your radio."

Jeeter sighed, rolled over into a corner and slipped

her headset on again. Reaching to her waist, she turned the dial of the radio.

I wish I knew what they're so excited about, Jeeter thought. But soon she was caught up in the music and was again wiggling and happily snapping her fingers.

FOUR

The First Message

Jeeter woke up to Monday morning and groaned. She hated Monday because Monday meant school and she already knew she wasn't allowed to take her radio with her.

"I'll only listen during recess!" she'd promised her mother.

But Mrs. Huff remained firm. "You'll play with your friends during recess." she said. "Come on now, Jeet, be reasonable. School is for sharing work and play. Not for staying by yourself listening to a radio."

Grumpily, Jeeter took her skateboard with her so she could zoom home to her music the minute school was out.

Which she did. She was the first Huff home.

She quickly changed into a pair of shorts, whipped the headset off Mason's ears, kissed his bald head and, plunking on her sunhat, zipped out the door.

She skateboarded, walked and skipped around Big Beaver's residential streets, stopped to play a lone game of hopscotch on a chalk outline someone had drawn on the sidewalk and wondered, after a while, what time it was.

"It's four o'clock, my little music lovers," the W-HIZ disc jockey said loudly in her ear, "and we're going to break now for the news! Back in five with the faves!"

"Ah," Jeeter said to herself. "Four o'clock. Better go home before I get yelled at . . ." She hopped back onto her skateboard and began to speed down the sidewalk as a commercial began on her station. Commercials usually bored Jeeter. This one, with a mom talking to her little boy, was no different— until she heard the little boy's name: Mason.

MOM: Mason, what's that toothpaste you're using?

Mason! Jeeter thought. That sure is a coincidence . . .

BOY: This yellow stuff, Mom!

MOM: But, Mason—
that toothpaste doesn't
contain fluoride. You
should be using *Brite*.
It's better for your teeth
and it tastes like rasp-
berry-mint!

BOY: Mmmmm! It
does taste good, Mom!

Jeeter smiled to herself
as she skated along.
"You're crazy, Mason,"
she said out loud. "*Brite*
stinks."

MOM: I told you so,
Mason. Now, run along
and play . . .

And then the little boy on the radio said, "*Watch
the bike, Jeeter!*"

Without thinking about it, Jeeter swerved quickly
to her left, and as she did, a teen-age boy on a ten-
speed whizzed past her, missing her by inches. He
was yelling something at her over his shoulder, but
she couldn't hear him because her headset was on.

Jeeter's jaw dropped. *Her headset was on*!

She had sprawled onto the grass near the curb
when the bike went by, but she hadn't even felt the
fall. She just sat there with her mouth open.

Watch the bike, Jeeter!

Someone had said it. Someone had said it on the radio!

Jeeter pushed her knuckle against her front teeth and frowned.

Someone on the radio had warned her about the bike, which she'd never have noticed with her head-set on.

The commercial, she thought. A mom and her son. Her son named Mason. Doing a toothpaste commercial. During the toothpaste commercial, the little boy had said: *"Watch the bike, Jeeter!"*

Jeeter sat cross-legged on the grass. She propped her elbows on her knees and rested her head against her fists. She listened very hard to her radio, still at the same station, W-HIZ. But the commercial was over. There was another commercial, this one for zit medicine, and then the DJ came back and played another record. Jeeter listened and listened. There were more commercials and more records, but none with a mom and little boy, and no one named Mason and no one who spoke her name.

Jeeter scratched her head and stood up. It was only then that she felt shaky. Her legs were rubbery, and she could feel her heart pounding. She had nearly been in an accident, but something saved her. She took a deep breath and blew it out. Then she picked up her skateboard and walked the rest of the way home. Slowly. And on the grass, not the sidewalk.

Carol-Ann was in the kitchen when Jeeter came in, still shaky. She was putting some baking potatoes into the oven.

"Where were you?" she asked.

Jeeter answered with a question of her own. "Where's Mom?"

"She called. She'll be a little late." Mrs. Huff was a dental hygienist, and her appointments were arranged so that she could be home by four o'clock most days. "Were you out with that radio?" Carol-Ann said.

"Yeah . . ." The headset was resting on Jeeter's neck.

"You better be careful, Jeeter. I'm not kidding. You don't hear anything when you're wearing that and you could get hurt."

"I know," Jeeter said softly.

"What do you mean? Did something happen?" Carol-Ann closed the oven door and looked at her sister. "Boy, Jeeter, you're white as a ghost, you know that? What happened?"

Jeeter opened her mouth. "I—" she began.

Carol-Ann waited.

"I was listening—I heard—" Jeeter stammered, then stopped.

"What?" Carol-Ann asked impatiently.

"Uh, nothing," Jeeter said finally. "Nothing happened."

Carol-Ann made a face. "Let's have it," she said.

Jeeter tried again. "The radio—" she said.

"What about the radio?"

Jeeter looked into Carol-Ann's face. She could almost feel the words forming in her throat. *A little boy on the radio named Mason warned me about a speeding bike!* The very words were in her mouth! Now they were on her lips! Now the words were coming out!

"Nothing!" Jeeter yelled, and Carol-Ann jumped back from the force.

"Okay, okay," Carol-Ann said. "Forget it."

Jeeter wanted to listen to her radio during dinner. Her mother and father said no. Jeeter pleaded. She said she really wanted to hear the commercials, not the music.

Her mother and father said no.

Carol-Ann said, "Oh, wow, that's a new one!"

Jeeter said, "Just this once!"

Her mother and father said no.

Jeeter sat quietly through dinner and picked at her food.

"Honestly, Jeeter, I'm beginning to be sorry we gave you that radio," her mother said. "What happened to your happy smile? You used to bubble all evening! Now look at you!"

Jeeter panicked. They might take the radio away! She began to smile and bubble.

That night, very late, she crept into her parents' room. Her mother was sound asleep, but her father was awake and reading a book.

"Daddy . . ." Jeeter whispered.

Her father patted the side of his bed. Jeeter sat down.

"I want to ask you something," Jeeter said.

"Okay," he said softly. "If you whisper, your mom won't wake up. What is it?"

"Can somebody really talk to you on the radio?"

"What?"

Jeeter repeated it.

"Isn't that what they do on the radio?" her father asked. "Talk to you?"

"No, I mean . . . to *me*. To me. Jeeter."

"You mean . . . directly to you?"

Jeeter nodded.

"You mean . . . 'Hi, Jeeter, how are you?' "

Jeeter nodded.

"Well . . ." Her father scratched his chin. "I guess so . . . If you knew the announcer . . . or the disc jockey or whatever. Or maybe someone could call up the radio station and say, 'Please dedicate the next record to my friend Jeeter Huff . . .' Something like that . . . Is that what you mean?"

Jeeter wrinkled her nose and shook her head.

"Well, what *do* you mean?"

Jeeter's mother rolled over, and her father put a finger to his lips.

"I mean . . ." Jeeter said carefully, "suppose you were crossing the street."

"Uh-huh . . ."

"And . . . a car was coming but you didn't see it. And you were listening to the radio so you didn't hear the car."

"Okay . . ."

"Could the radio say, 'Hey, watch out for that car, Mister?' All of a sudden? Just like that?"

Mr. Huff's eyebrows went up.

"Could it?" Jeeter asked again.

"Jeeter, now how could a radio voice do that?" Her father was looking at her as if she'd lost her marbles. "Can a radio voice see you?"

"No . . ."

"Well, then how can a radio voice even know that you're crossing a street? Jeeter, this is really a silly conversation, isn't it?"

Jeeter sighed. If she said, "But, Daddy, it happened," she figured he'd probably wake up her mother and they'd both call Dr. Bronsky.

"I think," her father continued, "that you must have had a dream, don't you?"

Jeeter wanted to say, "But it was broad daylight!" Instead, she said, "Yeah, I guess I had a dream."

"Well, go right back to bed," her father said. "It's very late and you've got school in the morning."

Jeeter said, "Okay." Then she said, "Are you sure it isn't even a *little bit* possible?"

"Jeeter . . ."

"Okay, I'm going. Thanks, Daddy . . ."

"Any time," her father said, picking up his book.

Jeeter closed her parents' door and padded back toward her own room.

I should be picking up a book, too, she thought. I was so busy thinking about that kid on the radio I never even started my homework . . .

She went over to her little blue desk, sat down and took out her sheet of math problems. But after she had managed to finish three of them, she stopped again and nibbled on her pinky fingernail.

Sure, it was a dream, she told herself. It had to be. A daydream. Sure. That's all it was. She finished her homework.

FIVE

The Locket

Jeeter went to school the next day—Tuesday—but she still had some trouble concentrating. Claudia had to drag her outside to play at recess.

"Are you sure you're not sick?" Claudia asked.

"Yeah, I'm sure . . ."

"Because you look sick, if you ask me. I mean you don't look like *you*. You look kind of sad."

"I'm not sad," Jeeter said. "I was just thinking."

"It's recess," Claudia told her. "You're not supposed to think at recess. You're supposed to play. Let's play hide-and-seek. Let's get Patsy and Susan."

Jeeter shrugged and said, "Okay," but soon she

was playing the game as hard as the others: hiding in the woods in clumps of bushes, giggling when the "seeker" passed close to her, running like crazy for home-free-all. When the bell rang in the school-yard, the girls lay panting under a tree, red-faced and laughing.

"Guess you feel better," Claudia said as they got up.

Jeeter smiled a big smile. "Yup," she agreed. She had finally made up her mind that what had happened to her the day before really was a dream and she'd better forget it.

As they walked to the side door of the school, Claudia suddenly clutched at her throat. She gasped.

"What is it?" Jeeter asked.

"My locket's gone," Claudia said.

"The one you got for Christmas?"

Claudia nodded. "It's real gold. My mother told me not to wear it to school—she'll have a screaming fit!"

"But you didn't lose it on purpose," Jeeter said.

"It doesn't matter . . ." Claudia started to cry. "I'll get grounded for the rest of my life!"

"No, you won't."

"I will, I will!" Claudia wailed.

"Did you have it when we came out for recess?"

"I think so . . ."

"Okay, then after school we'll go over all the places we hid in and look for it," Jeeter promised.

They did, but they didn't find the locket. Claudia's face was red from crying. Finally, Jeeter said, "Come on. I'll walk you home."

"I'm not going home!" Claudia cried.

"Aw, sure you are, Claudia . . ."

"No! At least, not yet. Let's go over to your house . . . I'll stay there till dinner. Maybe I'll even stay for dinner."

Jeeter shrugged. "Okay," she said.

They walked together slowly. Now Claudia was the one who needed cheering up and Jeeter tried her best.

"Hey, look at that woolly dog, Claudia! Isn't he cute?"

Claudia grunted.

"Look, he's got a shoe in his mouth!"

Claudia, staring at the sidewalk, mumbled, "Uh-huh . . ."

"Look! There's a lady chasing the dog into the park! Look, Claudia! She's only wearing one shoe!"

Claudia sighed. "Mmmm," she said.

"Oh, now look! The lady's got the shoe back . . . Ha! Now the dog is chasing *her*! Look, Claudia!"

Jeeter grinned and pointed, but Claudia only nodded woefully. Jeeter patted her shoulder.

When they arrived at the Huffs', Jeeter fixed them a snack, which Claudia didn't eat. Then they went up to Jeeter's room, where Claudia flopped onto the rug, lay on her back and stared at the ceiling. Every now and then she moaned.

"I wish I could make you feel better like you did for me," Jeeter said. "How about listening to some music?" She reached for her little radio.

"No," Claudia said. "If I feel better now, I'll only feel worse later when I have to think about it again."

Jeeter shook her head. She took her headset from Mason's ears and listened to her radio by herself, lying on the rug next to Claudia and staring at the ceiling.

"Four o'clock, W-HIZ fans," the DJ said, "and time now for the news! Hang in, li'l darlings. Back in five with the faves! But first—this word."

The commercial began.

MOM: Now, Mason, you didn't buy the soap I asked for!

Jeeter's eyes widened. She sat up.

BOY: But, Mom . . . all soaps are the same.

MOM: No, they're not.
I asked you to get *Sof-tie*. It's the only one that
keeps my skin moist!
BOY: Really?
MOM: Yes, because it
contains Hydrozylene
3!

And then the little boy said, *"The locket's under
the drinking fountain near the gym, Jeeter! Hurry
up before the janitor sweeps!"*

MOM: . . . So, Ma-son, be sure to buy *Sof-tie* next time, all right?
In the pink-and-gold
wrapper.

Jeeter reached over and clutched Claudia's arm,
which was lying limp on the floor.

"Ow!" Claudia yelled, but Jeeter didn't hear her.
She was still wearing her headset.

"What's the matter?" Claudia whined, rubbing
her arm where Jeeter's nails had dug in.

Mason! Jeeter thought. She looked at the doll on
her bed. The bald little baby with the double chin
sat blank-faced, just where she had left him.

"What's the *matter*?" Claudia asked again. Loudly
this time.

"Sh!" Jeeter said, listening very hard. But the news was just ending and the disc jockey was coming back with music. Jeeter took off the headset and stood up.

"Let's go, Claudia," she said.

"Where?"

"Never mind, let's just go. Before the janitor sweeps!"

"Before the—" Claudia was saying, but Jeeter had hold of her hand and was dragging her down the stairs.

"Where are you two going?" Jeeter's mother called as they rushed out the front door, but Jeeter only said, "We'll be back in a minute!" over her shoulder.

"Where *are* we going?" Claudia asked, running to keep up with her friend, who was nearly flying.

"The school," Jeeter said.

"*Why?*"

"Never mind. There's just something I have to check out."

"What?"

"Never *mind*, Claudia, just run!"

"But what did you say about the janitor?"

Jeeter didn't answer.

They met the school janitor just inside the front door. He was holding a push broom.

Panting, Jeeter grabbed the broom from his hand.

"Hey—" he began.

"Did you sweep near the gym yet?" Jeeter asked.

"The gym? No, I was just on my way—"

"Thanks!" Jeeter cried, shoving the broom back at the astonished man. She raced down the hall, Claudia right behind her.

Jeeter stopped at the drinking fountain and got down on her knees. She peered all around the floor under the fountain. Her heart was pounding.

And there, under the water pipe just where it met the wall, was a tiny heart attached to a bunched gold chain.

Jeeter closed her eyes.

"What are you doing?" Claudia asked, standing above Jeeter with her hands on her hips.

Jeeter picked up the chain with two fingers and dangled the heart. She looked up at Claudia.

"Jeeter . . ." Claudia whispered.

"Well, take it," Jeeter said, still on her knees. "It's yours, isn't it?"

They all sat around the Huff dining room table: Jeeter, her parents, Carol-Ann and Claudia, who had stayed for dinner even though it was a school night.

"Tell me again," Mr. Huff said, frowning into his coffee. "Once more."

Jeeter sighed. "I told you four times," she said. "At first I really made up my mind that it was a dream. But this time, Claudia was there too. And how would I know where to look for the locket anyway? The little boy on the radio told me!"

"And his name is Mason," Carol-Ann said.

"Yeah!"

Claudia touched her locket. "See?" she said. "Here's the proof. Jeeter's radio is magic!"

Mrs. Huff shook her head back and forth.

"You know what I think?" Mr. Huff said, leaning back in his chair. "I think that maybe Jeeter remembered seeing you drop that locket, Claudia—"

"But I didn't!"

"No, wait. Maybe you didn't think you remembered, but when you were lying on the floor upstairs, Jeeter, it just came back to you."

Jeeter groaned.

"There has to be a logical explanation," Mr. Huff said. "There's just no such thing as a magic radio!"

"Jeeter, you always had a vivid imagination," Mrs. Huff said.

"No, I didn't," Jeeter said. "And I didn't imagine it, either. The little boy talked to me! He said to get there before the janitor sweeps!"

Carol-Ann snorted, riffling her paper napkin.

"*I* believe you, Jeeter," Claudia whispered.

"And this little boy talks to you all the time?" Carol-Ann asked with a smug face.

"No . . ." Jeeter answered seriously and licked her upper lip. "Not all the time . . . I got the radio on Friday and I listened all night—"

"All *night*?" her mother said.

Jeeter winced. "Well . . . almost . . . And he didn't talk to me then. Or Saturday . . . and I listened all day. Or Sunday, either. The first time was yesterday. Monday. When I got warned about the bike."

"That's why you came home looking so funny," Carol-Ann said. "And you wouldn't tell me."

"Would you have believed me?" Jeeter asked.

"Uh-uh," Carol-Ann said truthfully. "I'm not sure I do now, either."

"Monday," Mr. Huff repeated. "And then again today."

Jeeter nodded.

"But you were in school both days," Mrs. Huff said. "You didn't take your radio to school, did you?"

"No! You said I couldn't! I listened to it after school."

"Then it's right after school that you heard—you *thought* you heard—the little boy speak to you. Is that right?" her father said.

Jeeter thought. "Well . . . not *right* after school, because today I helped Claudia look in the woods for the locket. We didn't even get home till about three-thirty or maybe later . . . Wait a minute! It was four o'clock. Both days. I remember, it was time for the news on W-HIZ. It was the commercial that came on right before the news. Both days!"

"Okay, then," Carol-Ann said, getting up to clear the table. "That's easy enough. Tomorrow we'll *all* listen to your radio at four o'clock. Mom, can you get home?"

"Well, I suppose so . . ."

"Daddy?"

Mr. Huff smiled and shook his head. "No, but if all of you listen, I'm sure that'll be enough. You understand, Jeeter, it isn't that I don't believe you."

"Yes, it is."

"Well, but . . . it *is* pretty hard . . . a story like that . . . I mean, *magic*, Jeeter—"

"*I* believe it," Claudia said.

"Well, just don't tell anybody," Carol-Ann said. "They'll think Jeeter's crazy or something. I'd be so embarrassed!"

Jeeter wrinkled her nose at her sister and popped a cookie into her mouth.

"Don't forget," Carol-Ann said. "Everybody be right here in this kitchen at four o'clock tomorrow."

" ' . . . In this kitchen at four o'clock tomorrow,' " Jeeter mimicked in a tiny little voice, and everyone laughed except Carol-Ann.

SIX

Everybody Listens

Wednesday afternoon.

Jeeter and Claudia sat together at the Huffs' kitchen table, while across the room, Carol-Ann bobbed to the music on Jeeter's radio, which sat on the counter next to the sink.

"It's almost four, Jeeter," Claudia whispered. "Do you think your mom'll make it in time?"

Jeeter shrugged. "I guess . . ."

"What's the matter?"

Jeeter lifted her eyes toward Carol-Ann, who was now dancing as The Silver Bullets wailed "You're So Bad!"

"Aw, it's just Carol-Ann," Jeeter whispered back. "She never lets me do anything with her and her friends, but the first time anything nice happens to me, she butts right in."

"Mmm." Claudia looked over at Carol-Ann. "I don't have a big sister, but I guess they're probably all like that."

"Yeah. I wonder what she'll do when she hears that little boy talk to me on the radio . . ."

Claudia jumped up. "Here's your mom, Jeeter—"

The kitchen door opened and Mrs. Huff rushed in. "Did I make it?" she asked as she looked at the clock.

"Uh-huh," Carol-Ann said. "A few more minutes."

"You're So Bad" blared to its finish. The DJ screamed his praise. Then he said, "It's news time, babies. Back in—"

"Five with the faves!" Jeeter finished for him. "That's what he always says! 'Back in five with the faves!' "

"Sh!" Carol-Ann said, leaning closer to the radio. The DJ said, "And now this word."

Jeeter and Claudia clutched each other's hands.

"How many of you kids out there *really* start your day with a *good* breakfast?" It was a man's voice.

Jeeter looked at Claudia. "That's not—" she began, but Carol-Ann said, "Sh!"

"I mean," the voice went on, "a *good* breakfast!

Has your teacher told you that breakfast is the most important meal of the day? Well, it is—"

Jeeter was shaking her head. Carol-Ann held up her hand. "Don't talk," she whispered.

". . . So be sure you don't run out of the house in the morning, grabbing a doughnut or something quick just because you're in a hurry—"

"That's not it," Jeeter said, still shaking her head.

". . . This has been a public service announcement," the man finished, "because W-HIZ *cares* about you!"

"And now, the news," an announcer said. And the news began.

"Hmph," Carol-Ann sniffed. "I told you so, Jeeter," she said. "A little boy on the radio talks to you. Ha!" But she looked very disappointed.

"Well," Mrs. Huff said, "I guess that's that." She lifted Jeeter's chin with her fingers. "I'm sorry, honey. I'm still glad you have an imagination, though. Don't feel bad."

Jeeter wasn't sure what she felt. She watched Carol-Ann head for the living room. Mrs. Huff took off her white work shoes and put on the soft slippers she kept behind the kitchen door. "Why don't you and Claudia go play now?" she suggested.

Jeeter picked up her radio and started for the stairs with Claudia right behind her.

"What happened?" Claudia asked as they climbed.

"I don't know," Jeeter answered. "I really don't."

They reached Jeeter's room. Mason sat on the bed as usual with the headset over his ears, the blank expression fixed on his little round double-chinned face. Jeeter moved to place herself in front of his empty stare.

"What happened?" she asked the doll.

Claudia looked from Jeeter to Mason. "Do you really think he'll tell you?" she asked.

"I just can't figure it out, Claudia," Jeeter said. "I got this little message—from Mason—on Monday and yesterday at four o'clock. Right before the news on W-HIZ."

"Weekdays," Claudia said. "Not weekends."

"Uh-huh . . . weekdays."

"Weekdays . . ." Claudia muttered to herself and sat down on Jeeter's bed.

Jeeter began to pace the room.

"And today's a weekday. Wednesday. But it didn't happen today." She caught her lower lip between her teeth and frowned. "Hey, there was one other thing," she said.

"What?"

"I had the headset on both times. Hey, Claudia— I was wearing the headset!"

Claudia's face lit up. "That's right! The first time

you were on the skateboard and the second time you were with me. But both times you were wearing your phones!"

"That's right!"

"So what now, Jeeter? What do we do now?"

Jeeter grinned at her friend. "Now? Well, all we do now is come back here tomorrow at four o'clock and this time—this time, Claudia, we'll use the headset!"

"Well, but only one person can use a headset," Claudia said.

"I know. We'll put it on *you*!"

The Huffs were quiet at the supper table. Everyone was watching Mr. Huff, who had had a bad day at the office. Jeeter, who'd had a discouraging day herself, was trying to send him comforting thoughts across the table.

Mr. Huff poked a string bean with his fork, but he didn't pick it up. Then he cut a piece of pot roast but that, too, remained on his plate.

"Try to eat, dear," Mrs. Huff said. "Things will work out tomorrow. I'm sure they will."

"Not with Rumplemeyer, they won't!" Mr. Huff grumped. "He's going to ruin the whole project. How he ever got to be a supervisor I'll never know!"

Jeeter reached across and put her small hand over her father's large one.

"Don't you worry, Daddy," she said. "You always make the projects come out all right, even though Mr. Rumplemeyer's the supervisor."

Mr. Huff smiled a little. "Now how would you know that?" he asked.

"Because," Jeeter answered, still holding his hand, "on the last two projects you stayed late at work and didn't come home for dinner. And the next day you said Mr. Williams liked the way you finished both of them. I remember because we all missed you at supper."

"Aw, Jeet," her father said and patted her hand. "I'm afraid it's different this time. Cary Rumplemeyer's messed this one up so badly there's not much I can do about it." Mr. Huff shook his head. "But I'll get the blame. I had the idea for it in the first place."

"No, you won't, Daddy," Carol-Ann said. "If it's not your fault you won't get the blame."

Jeeter got up from her place, walked behind her father's chair and hugged him around the neck. It always bothered her when anyone in the family was unhappy—even Carol-Ann.

Mr. Huff squeezed Jeeter's arm and said, "Sweet Jeet."

SEVEN

A Missed Message

Thursday. Jeeter and Claudia raced each other to the Huffs' house, giggling nervously.

"But we have time!" Claudia called to her friend, who was dancing ahead of her. "We're going to be so early and then we'll just be sitting around your room chewing our nails and waiting!"

"I know," Jeeter said, "but I want to be out of Carol-Ann's way before she guesses what we're doing. Come on!"

Carol-Ann wasn't home when the arrived and they scurried upstairs.

"Hi, Mason!" Jeeter called to the doll on the bed.

Claudia stared hard at him. "Hi, Mason," she said

softly. Jeeter smiled at her. "Jeeter, do you really think it's the doll talking?"

Jeeter shrugged. "The name's the same," she said. She sat on her bed and plopped Mason onto her lap. "You're a strange baby," she said, hugging him.

"A real strange baby," Claudia agreed.

"Let's turn on the radio," Jeeter said, "and when it's time, I'll give you the headset." She turned the dial and the radio blared the middle section of The Elephant Herd's hit single, "Rattle Your Gourds."

They listened to the music together, but this time, Jeeter took no pleasure in it. She was waiting until four o'clock. She wondered what the message would be, if there was any at all.

At 3:55, she took the headset from Mason's ears. "Let's plug it in," she told Claudia anxiously. "It's almost time. Now as soon as the commercial starts, you hold up your hand so I'll know you're getting it, okay?"

Claudia nodded and put the headset on.

"Is it okay?" Jeeter said loudly.

Claudia nodded.

"Want me to turn it up?"

Claudia shook her head.

"Can you hear clearly?"

Claudia nodded.

"What are they saying?"

"Jeeter, be qui-et!"

Jeeter got quiet. She hugged Mason's soft stuffed body tightly. She watched Claudia.

" 'Back in five with the faves,' " Claudia mouthed to let Jeeter know the DJ was saying his usual line. Jeeter nodded.

Claudia's mouth opened slightly. Her face was expectant. Jeeter squeezed her fingers together in a fist. She waited for Claudia's hand to be raised.

After a moment, Claudia pulled the headset off and handed it to Jeeter.

"What?" Jeeter cried. *"What?"*

"It's nothing. Nothing at all. Just another public service announcement. About summer jobs for teenagers—"

Jeeter quickly put the small orange phones to her own ears and listened intently.

". . . *with Rumplemeyer,"* she heard. *"Tune in tomorrow, Jeeter."* And then the news came on.

"Claudia!" Jeeter cried. "There *was* something! There was! Didn't you hear it?"

"No," Claudia said. "There wasn't anything."

"But there *was*! Mason just said 'Rumplemeyer'!"

Claudia glanced at the doll and then at Jeeter. "What's a Rumplemeyer?" she asked.

"Didn't you hear it?" Jeeter wailed. "There was a message!" She turned the doll in her lap so that she could study his face. "You know what?" she asked.

"Are you talking to me or—or him?" Claudia asked, nodding at Mason.

Jeeter looked at her. "I think it only works for me."

Claudia folded her hands in her lap. "I guess so, Jeeter. I guess it only works for you. *If* it works . . ."

"What do you mean, *if* it works?" Jeeter asked.

"Well, I had the headset on," Claudia said, "and I didn't hear anything about a Rumplemeyer. I didn't get any message. None at all! Maybe it's all in your head, Jeeter."

"It is not! What about your locket?"

"I'm glad you found my locket! But I never heard anybody say anything over your radio!" Claudia stood up.

"And I missed the whole message because you didn't hear anything on my radio!" Jeeter stood up.

"I think I'd better go home!" Claudia said.

"I think you'd better, too!" Jeeter shouted.

As she listened to Claudia stomp down the stairs, Jeeter flopped onto her bed again.

"Nothing's working," she said to Mason. "Dad's in a big mess, Claudia's mad, I missed the message about Rumplemeyer . . ." She frowned. There was something else, she thought. One more thing . . .

And then she remembered. The boy on the radio had said, "Tune in tomorrow."

EIGHT

Nobody Listens

Jeeter fidgeted in school. She managed to complete her work, but only after a few pauses and frowns from Mrs. Bonino.

After school, Claudia smiled to show she wanted to make up and asked Jeeter to play. Jeeter smiled back. They were friends again, but Jeeter didn't want to play. She wanted to get home as fast as she could, so she waved at Claudia and hurried away.

She rushed through the back door, panting, and found a note with her name on it stuck to the refrigerator door with a magnet shaped like a strawberry. She read out loud:

" 'Lulu and I are going shopping. If you absolutely

positively need me for something really important, we'll be trying on bathing suits at Klemperer's. Or we might be at the doughnut shop. Or The Gap. Or the drug store. Love, C-A.' "

Oh, good! Jeeter thought. She'll be gone the whole afternoon.

Jeeter looked at the note. "No, Carol-Ann," she said, "I absolutely positively won't need you for something really important."

She went up to her room, took the radio and headset, pinched Mason's stuffed cheek, then ran downstairs and outside. The best place for complete privacy, she decided, was behind the house, near the garage.

The dial was already set at W-HIZ. Jeeter put on the headset and listened and waited. It was only 3:20. She had forty minutes to look forward to her special commercial.

The music was loud and many of the songs were Jeeter's favorites—her "faves," as the DJ said—but this time she didn't tap her feet, snap her fingers or bounce on the grass. This time she listened hard. She closed her eyes to listen harder—and fell asleep.

She woke with a start and gasped out loud, terrified she'd missed it! But she exhaled heavily with relief when she heard the disc jockey say, "We'll hear the news after this smash single by that brand new group that's fast climbing to the top of the charts! And here it is, li'l darlings! Let's boogie down now! It's 'Barefoot in the Mud' by Sore Throat, featuring Dougy Mush!"

Whew, Jeeter thought. I'm just in time. She looked up at her bedroom window as if she expected to see Mason sitting there, waving at her. But there was no one in the window. And suddenly the DJ was back on.

"All-ll *right*, li'l darlings, don't you love Dougy Mush and Sore Throat!" he said, and Jeeter mouthed with him, "Back in five with the faves!"

Jeeter adjusted the headset and held her breath.

MOM: Mason, I see you're feeding Skippy the same old dog food.

BOY: Yes, Mom. But he doesn't seem to like it any more.

MOM: Well, Mason, let's try this new food I just bought. It's called *Chomp*.

BOY: *Chomp?*

MOM: That's right. *Chomp*. Let's just pour it out of the bag into his

bowl and see what he
does!

And then the little boy said, *"Jeeter, tell your dad
not to worry. On Monday he's due for a promotion.
Rumplemeyer's going to have a big fight with the
boss and quit."*

MOM: Now, Mason,
just look at that dog eat!
BOY: He loves it,
Mom! Let's buy *Chomp*
from now on!

Jeeter took off her headset with shaking hands.
She'd barely heard the last two lines of the commercial, though she had paid attention in case there
was anything more just for her.

Rumplemeyer's going to quit, she said to herself.
He's going to fight with Mr. Williams and—

Suddenly, she could hear her own mom calling
to her from inside the house. She tried to get up,
but she found her legs were shaky, too, so she sat
still on the grass in the yard, breathing quickly, as
the W-HIZ news came on.

It wasn't until long afterward that Jeeter had a chance
to be alone with her father. He had a headache, she
could tell. He was sitting on the couch, just gazing

into space. The sports section of Friday's paper lay open on his lap.

"Daddy?" Jeeter began. She was trembling with excitement.

"Hi, there, Sweet Jeet."

"I really love you, Daddy." She couldn't wait to tell him!

"I love you, too, honey."

"And everything's going to be all right for you. I promise!"

Mr. Huff clicked his teeth together. "Thanks, Jeet," he said.

"Daddy . . . I heard on my radio . . ."

"Now, Jeeter—"

She knelt beside him on the couch. "I did! I did! On my radio, Daddy. Let me tell you what's going to happen!"

"Jeeter, honey—Listen to me now . . . I think it's nice to have imaginary friends."

Jeeter said, "But—"

"Don't interrupt me," her father said, looking at her. "As I said, I think it's nice to have imaginary friends. I had one myself, as a matter of fact. When I was just about your age, too."

"You did?"

"I did. It was a horse. A beautiful white stallion who would speed to my rescue and carry me away on his back as soon as I ran into any trouble. His name was Condor."

"Wow," Jeeter breathed. "I didn't know that, Daddy."

"It's true. Every time that big kid Gerson Potter waited for me at the corner of my street to beat me up, I used to whisper, 'Con-dor . . . Con-dor! Come fly me away!' "

"And what happened?" Jeeter asked excitedly.

"I got a black eye and a nosebleed from Gerson Potter."

"Condor didn't come? He didn't rescue you?"

Mr. Huff took her hand in his own.

"No, Jeet, Condor didn't come. He was only in my head. That's the only place he lived."

Jeeter looked down at the flowered print of the couch. "Okay, Daddy . . ." she said. Her father began to get up, but Jeeter held tight to his hand, keeping him at her level. "Just one thing," she said.

"What is it, honey?"

She said it quickly. "On Monday Mr. Rumplemeyer is going to have a big fight with Mr. Williams and he's going to quit and you're going to get his job!"

Now, Mr. Huff stood up. Very tall.

"Jeeter, this has gone far enough."

"I won't say another word," Jeeter said.

"See that you don't," her father said.

Jeeter left the room with her head down. She bumped right into Carol-Ann, who was flying down the stairs carrying an overstuffed gym bag.

"Ouch! Jeeter, watch where you're going!"

"Sorry," Jeeter mumbled. Then she noticed the bag. "Where are *you* going?" she asked.

"To Lulu's. She's having a slumber party. Oh, and by the way . . . I borrowed your blue shirt. It fits after all."

"Well, boy, Carol-Ann—" Jeeter began, but Carol-Ann had rushed out. Jeeter made a face. "What would you say if I borrowed something of *yours* without permission?" she said to the closed door. "Boy!" she said again, and slumped down to sit in a heap on the stairs.

NINE

Jeeter Is Right

Monday was warm and sunny. Jeeter's behavior in school was worse than it had been on Friday. She raised her hand in math and forgot her answer. She forgot the capital of Nebraska. She lost a sneaker in gym, and she forgot her change at the ice-cream line in the cafeteria. She was thinking about her father at his office. She was wondering what time the fight would start. Most of all she was trying to picture the look on her father's face when Mr. Williams called him in to tell him he had been promoted to supervisor. She was deep into all this thought when she heard her teacher call her name.

"Yes, Mrs. Bonino?" Jeeter said quickly.

"This—is—the—third—time—I—have—called—

your—name, Jeeter Huff," her teacher said. "You have been in a daze since last Friday. And you haven't heard one word of what's gone on in this classroom since you walked in here this morning."

Jeeter blushed pink and red.

"I'm going to nip this spring fever in the bud before it goes any further," Mrs. Bonino said crisply. "You have detention this afternoon, young lady. You will stay with me in this room, doing all the work you missed, until four o'clock."

"Did you say four o'clock?" Jeeter squeaked.

"Do I have to repeat myself again?" the teacher barked.

Jeeter shook her head.

Mrs. Bonino sat at her desk, correcting papers.

Jeeter sat at her desk, writing on one of the papers to be corrected. She couldn't concentrate on it. Four o'clock, she thought. I'll miss my commercial. I won't get any message from Mason. How will I know what's happening? I have to get home by four. What if something happens that I need to tell Daddy?

Jeeter tapped her pencil absent-mindedly. Mrs. Bonino looked up. Jeeter grabbed the pencil tip with her other hand as if to silence it. Mrs. Bonino went back to her work.

Jeeter was supposed to write her spelling words

in sentences. There were twenty words. Jeeter had used four.

Four. Four o'clock.

She raised her hand.

"Yes?" Mrs. Bonino peered down at her.

"May I please leave at quarter-to, Mrs. Bonino?" Jeeter asked. "I promise I'll do all the work tonight for homework . . ."

"I'm sorry, Jeeter. I said you'll work here until four."

"But, please, Mrs. Bonino . . ." Jeeter crossed her fingers under her desk. "I have a dentist appointment at four. My mother'll be waiting for me. I'll mess up their whole schedule if I'm late . . . My mother doesn't like to get home much past four and today I'm getting my teeth cleaned and—"

"Now, Jeeter," her teacher interrupted, "Dr. Brownmiller's office is right over on the next block. It will take you three minutes to walk there from here. It's closer than from your own house. I will allow you to leave at exactly three minutes to four."

"But—"

"And not a minute sooner. Get to work."

Why didn't I say a *doctor's* appointment? Jeeter asked herself angrily. Dr. Bronsky's office is *three* blocks away and I could have left *ten* minutes earlier. She wrote three more spelling words in one sentence: "I like the wild, *woolly monster* who lives in the *basement*." Then she watched the clock.

As soon as the big hand clicked in at three minutes before the hour, Jeeter was on her feet.

"No more of this behavior tomorrow, Jeeter," Mrs. Bonino said while staring down at her work. But Jeeter was out the door, tearing as fast as she could from the building and down the street.

I'll never make it, she thought. Never. But maybe if—she was pushing hard now—if I run as fast as I ever did in my life, maybe—maybe—

She knew she made it home in record time. She threw open the front door and without bothering to close it, raced up the stairs to her room. I made it, she thought, I did it! She grabbed the headset from the doll and put it over one ear with one hand while the other hand turned on the radio. Then she adjusted the headset and fell panting to the floor.

"Our headline story this afternoon," a man's voice said, "is, of course, the malfunction in Air Force One, delaying the President's departure for—"

Jeeter ripped off the headset and banged her fist on the side of the bed. "Oh, *rats*!" she said aloud. "I'm too late!"

Jeeter sat waiting for her father to come home. She

didn't want the snack her mother offered, and she didn't want to hear Carol-Ann's chatter about a boy she and Lulu both liked. Mrs. Huff tried to talk to Jeeter about certain hormonal changes that take place in a young girl's body, but Jeeter didn't want to hear that either. She wanted her father to get home and tell her what had happened at the office.

He came home at 6:15 with three bunches of flowers.

The biggest bunch was for Jeeter.

"I'm sorry, Jeet—I just couldn't believe you. You really heard that on your radio?" Mr. Huff asked, when the excitement of his promotion had died down.

Jeeter nodded.

"If it was just a promotion she'd imagined—" Mr. Huff said to his wife. "But the fight between Rumplemeyer and Williams—you could hear it all over the office. I didn't know Rumplemeyer knew words like that!"

"And then what?" Mrs. Huff asked.

"Well, then, while we could all hear Rumplemeyer cleaning out his desk and slamming drawers, Dan Williams comes barging out of his office into mine, bellowing, 'Morton, start moving your things into the office down the hall'—meaning Rumplemeyer's—'It's got a window in it!' he yells. 'You've got a promotion and a raise, starting now!' And then he storms back into his own office." Mr. Huff looked down. "Just like Jeeter said," he added softly.

"My goodness," his wife breathed.

"Congratulations again, Daddy," Carol-Ann said.

"Thanks, honey."

Carol-Ann put her arm around her sister's shoulders. "Jeeter," she said in her ear, "could I talk to you privately for a minute?"

"Sure." Jeeter smiled up at Carol-Ann, and together they went upstairs, leaving their parents shaking their heads in the living room.

Carol-Ann pulled Jeeter into her bedroom and slammed the door behind them.

"Listen, Jeeter," she said, pushing Jeeter further into the room, "I believe you."

"Thanks a lot."

"Well, you have to admit it was hard to before."

"I wasn't lying," Jeeter said.

"I know, I never said you were lying. I just thought you had an—"

"I know, an 'active imagination.' That's what everybody said."

"Well, that's not lying."

"I don't see the difference," Jeeter muttered.

"Well, never mind, that's not what I wanted to talk to you about."

"What did you want to talk to me about?"

"Well . . . Do you think . . . Listen, I know this sounds funny . . ."

Jeeter didn't say anything. She let Carol-Ann fumble around.

"I mean . . . Well, what I mean is . . . Look, Jeeter, do you think you could ask that radio of yours—"

"I don't *ask* the radio *anything*," Jeeter interrupted. "It talks to *me*, I don't get to talk to *it*."

"Okay, okay. But it seems that if you want to know something, the radio tells you, right?"

Jeeter shrugged. "Sometimes, I guess. I did want to know where Claudia's locket was . . ."

"Right. Well, maybe you could want to know if Robbie Goldstein likes Lulu or me."

"Who's Robbie Goldstein?"

"He's this cute ninth grader. He winked at Lulu in the halls, but he *talked* to *me*. He plays lacrosse."

"Maybe he doesn't like either of you."

"Listen, smarty, I didn't ask *you*. I want to know from the radio. Some of the girls are getting letter-sweaters from their boyfriends on the teams and those sweaters are gorgeous and I want one."

Jeeter wriggled her toes. "I don't ask any questions, Carol-Ann . . . I just listen."

"Well . . ." Carol-Ann looked around, though no one was there in her bedroom with its closed door except herself and Jeeter. "Look, Jeeter . . . could you ask, uh, Mason?"

"What?"

"Could—you—ask—the—doll," Carol-Ann repeated. "I can't believe I'm even saying this, I'm so embarrassed."

Jeeter smiled at her sister and shook her head. "Boy, Carol-Ann," she said. "I think you should go talk to Dr. Bronsky. Mason's a doll, he's a newborn baby Cabbage Patch Kid. He doesn't talk, Carol-Ann. He's made of rubber and cloth—"

"O-kay, Jeeter, I get the message. Just see what you can do."

"I just listen," Jeeter said.

Carol-Ann Again

Jeeter's work improved so much on Tuesday that Mrs. Bonino complimented her, smiled at her and chose her for paper monitor.

"You see how that detention helped you?" Mrs. Bonino asked Jeeter. "If I hadn't brought you right back to earth, young lady, you would have dreamed away the entire spring, wouldn't you?"

Jeeter crossed her fingers behind her back and smiled. "Yes, Mrs. Bonino," she said. But Jeeter knew her improvement was really due to her father's relief and happiness.

That afternoon, Jeeter did stay in the schoolyard to

play with Claudia and Patsy and Susan, but she made sure she was home in plenty of time for the four o'clock news on her radio. She'd missed it the day before because of her detention, and even though things turned out well enough, she didn't want to miss another message as well.

But her radio wasn't in her room.

Mason sat on her bed, still wearing the headset over his stuffed ears and staring straight ahead. Jeeter frowned at him. Did the black pupils of his eyes seem wider or was it just the angle at which she was standing?

"Where's the radio, Mason?" Jeeter asked, but she knew he wouldn't answer. She didn't need an answer, anyway. She stalked down the hall to Carol-Ann's room. The door was closed, but she could hear the W-HIZ disc jockey through it.

"Okay, Carol-Ann, let's have my radio back," Jeeter called as she knocked loudly on the door. "Come on . . . I know you have it."

"You have it every day," Carol-Ann called back. "Let me have it—just today!"

Out in the hall, Jeeter tapped her foot impatiently.

"It won't do you any good, Carol-Ann," she said. "It won't talk to you."

There was a pause. Then the door was pulled open. Carol-Ann stood there holding the doorknob with one hand while pressing the little radio to her ear with the other.

"What do you mean, it won't talk to me? *Did you tell it not to talk to me, Jeeter?*"

Jeeter put her hands behind her back and rocked on her heels.

"Nope," she answered. "It just won't. That time we were all in the kitchen and everyone was waiting—remember? It didn't talk. And when Claudia wore the headset, it wouldn't talk to her, either. It only talks to me. I don't tell it anything. That's the truth!"

"Is it the headset?" Carol-Ann cried. "Is that it?"

Jeeter looked at the clock in the hall. It was five minutes to four.

"I don't ask any questions!" she said impatiently. "I don't know what it is, or why it talks to me, but it does!" She reached up and tried to grab the radio from her sister's hand, but Carol-Ann slammed her door again. "Give it to me, Carol-Ann!" Jeeter cried.

"In a minute!" Carol-Ann called back through the door.

"In a minute it'll be over and I'll miss it!" Jeeter cried.

But the door stayed closed and Carol-Ann wouldn't open it again until the W-HIZ newscaster announced the headlines.

"Here," Carol-Ann said, pushing the radio at Jeeter.

"What did you hear?" Jeeter asked.

"Just a stupid commercial."

"What for?"

"A car."

"Was there a little boy and his mother talking?"

Carol-Ann frowned. "No, it was a loud announcer and a singing group and a talking hatchback. Thanks for nothing, Jeeter!" She slammed her door.

Jeeter looked at the closed door, looked at her radio, looked again at the door.

"How come you're mad at *me*?" she yelled to Carol-Ann in her room. "*You're* the one who took *my* radio! And without permission!"

But Carol-Ann didn't answer, so Jeeter stuck out her tongue at the closed door and marched back to her own room. She flopped onto her bed and sat Mason on her lap.

"Carol-Ann doesn't get it, Mason," she said seriously to the doll. And then she added, "I'm not sure I do, either . . ."

ELEVEN

"Thank You, Mason."

When Jeeter got home from school the next day, she found Carol-Ann, Lulu and four or five other eighth-grade girls—all Carol-Ann's friends. They pounced on Jeeter as soon as she came through the door, which both annoyed and flattered her.

"Let's *see* the radio, Jeeter—"

"Let's see the headset!"

"*I* want to see the doll. What's his name?"

The questions all flew at once.

"It's just a plain-looking radio," Jeeter said. "And just a regular-looking headset . . . with earphones and wires . . ."

"How about the *doll?*" Cindy Stokes said in Jeeter's face. "Carol-Ann says it comes through the *doll*."

"I never said that," Jeeter said, frowning at Carol-Ann. "It's just that—well—the boy in the commercial has the same name as my—as the—oh, gosh, Carol-Ann . . ."

"Oh, come on, Jeeter. Wasn't I the one who gave you the headset? For your birthday? Well, wasn't I? And remember how you thanked me and everything?"

Jeeter repeated, "Oh, gosh, Carol-Ann," and shuffled her feet.

"So I figured, since you were so grateful, you could show it by sharing a little. I mean, if the radio only talks to you, then we'll just have to use you as a middleman."

"A middleman?"

"That's right," Lulu said. "We ask you the questions we want answers for and you go ask the radio. It's only fair, Jeeter, since it won't talk to Carol-Ann."

"But I don't know why it only talks to me," Jeeter said, "and I never ask it any questions!"

"Oh, but Jeeter—" one of the girls said, "think of what we can find out! We can know in advance when we're going to get a quiz and what the boys are thinking and—"

"—and who'll be the next President!" Lulu cried. "Now how about *that*!"

"Or we could bet on horse races," Cindy said, "or lottery numbers!"

Jeeter began to chew her thumbnail. She'd always dreamed of being included in Carol-Ann's group of big girls. Now she was in the middle of it all, the center of attention, and she wasn't having a very good time.

"You know what *I* think," she said finally, interrupting someone's question about a future husband, "*I* think you're going to jinx it. If you make me ask those things I bet it goes away."

"It won't go away," Lulu said smugly. "It's your magic genie, Jeeter, and you can make it do anything you want."

"No, I can't," Jeeter said, backing toward the door. "I never did—"

"Wait a minute," Carol-Ann said, holding up her hand. "Just wait a minute. What did you just say, Lulu? Just now, just before?"

"I said that Jeeter could make it do anything she wanted . . ."

"No," Carol-Ann said, "not that. About a genie. Isn't that it? A magic genie? Like in a bottle?"

Lulu nodded, bewildered.

"That's it!" Carol-Ann cried and clapped her hands

together. "Jeeter, what was it you wished for on your birthday? When you blew out the candles?"

Jeeter said, "Huh?"

"Come on, Jeeter. What was it?"

Jeeter felt her neck grow hot. "A fairy god-mother," she mumbled.

"What?" Carol-Ann said. "Louder."

"A fairy godmother!" Jeeter blurted angrily. "So what?"

"So," Carol-Ann said, folding her arms, "you *got* it."

"You mean," one of the girls said, "your sister made a wish on her birthday cake for a *fairy god-mother*? And that's what she got?"

Carol-Ann nodded and smirked. "That's right. Just like in *Cinderella*! Only these are modern times, and I'm not a wicked stepsister. So Jeeter's fairy godmother is a Cabbage Patch Kid named Mason who talks to her through a radio."

Jeeter thought Carol-Ann was behaving *just* like a wicked stepsister in a story, but she didn't say so. Instead, she merely lowered her eyelids a little and looked at Carol-Ann's friends, who had begun to argue.

"No, no, no," Lulu was saying. "That can't be right. If Jeeter told her wish, then that means it won't come true. Everyone knows that."

"Well, it *did* come true," Carol-Ann said, hands-on-hips. "And my father's promotion is living proof of it! And so is Claudia Sykes!"

"Well, then," Cindy said, "as long as it's a fairy godmother, even if it *is* inside a radio, then Jeeter gets to make wishes!"

Jeeter had heard enough. The girls weren't even looking at her now, only at each other with angry faces, so she slipped behind the group and climbed as quietly as she could up the stairs to her room and quickly closed the door behind her.

"Whew!" she sighed to Mason as she slipped the headset off him. "I had to get away! I really did! They won't leave me alone, Mason. They want me to—"

She was stopped by the sound of knocking on her door.

"Come on, Jeeter, open up!" It was Carol-Ann. And probably all those girls!

Jeeter put on the headset and turned the dial.

"It's time," she whispered to herself. "It's just time now! Four o'clock." She turned up the volume. I'll make it loud, she thought. Loud enough so I won't hear them. That's a good way to escape!

MOM: My poor boy!
What a terrible cough!
BOY: (cough, cough)

MOM: Here you are, Mason. Take some of this cough syrup. It's called *Coat-Your-Throat*.

BOY: Noo-ooo! I don't want any cough syrup! I hate cough medicine!

MOM: But *Coat-Your-Throat* is different, Mason. It not only takes away that nagging cough, it also tastes like candy!

BOY: It tastes like candy?

MOM: It sure does. Now open your mouth . . . wider . . .

And then the little boy said, "*Want to get away, Jeeter? Want to escape? All you have to do is close your eyes . . . Close your eyes, Jeeter, close your eyes . . .*"

MOM: Good!

Jeeter closed her eyes. She didn't hear the rest of the commercial. She didn't hear anything. Except . . .

Water.

The sound of water.

Lapping waves, soft . . . soft . . . and right nearby! So nearby, that the waves seemed to be right underneath her. As a matter of fact, they *were* underneath her!

Jeeter opened her eyes. And her mouth. She was in a small green rowboat, just big enough for her alone. It was rocking slightly on the water of a beautiful, calm, blue lake in a place Jeeter had never seen before. And it was surrounded on all sides by a valley with the greenest grass and the brightest wildflowers that Jeeter was sure ever grew anywhere.

"This is a magic place," Jeeter breathed. "A really truly magic place!"

She looked all around her and listened carefully. There were no sounds of angry voices or knocking on doors. There wasn't any Carol-Ann or Lulu or Cindy or *anyone*, except—Jeeter . . . and a small boat . . . and waves licking up . . . and an absolutely cloudless sky.

"Thank you, Mason," Jeeter breathed. "Thank you very much."

Jeeter opened her eyes and found herself on the floor of her room. Her headset was still on and there was loud rock music in her ears. She blinked. The sunlight was still coming through her window, but it was later now. She felt it. She took off the headset and heard her mother downstairs, calling her to dinner. Jeeter sat up.

Mason was lying next to her on the floor, face down. She picked him up, put him on the bed and fit the headset on him.

"I don't know, Mason," she said, shaking her head. "Was that a dream? It didn't feel like a dream. I don't remember sleeping . . ." And then, as her mother called again, she hurried out of the room and down the stairs.

TWELVE

Questions
and Answers

The next day, Jeeter refused to let her mind wander. She concentrated very hard on her work and received another compliment from Mrs. Bonino.

"Is it your magic radio that's helping you do better in school, Jeeter?" Claudia teased during recess.

"Nope," Jeeter answered. "I just *tried* harder."

"Oh, *that*," Claudia said with a sigh. "That means *work*."

"That's right," Jeeter said and giggled.

"Want to come over after school? My brother put up a basketball hoop over the garage."

Jeeter hesitated. It sounded like fun. And she didn't want to run into Carol-Ann's friends again, all ganging up on her in her living room. Still, she wanted to be home by four . . .

"Maybe just for half an hour," she told Claudia.

Jeeter was red-faced and sweaty by the time she arrived home. She slipped in through the kitchen door, hoping to avoid a bunch of clamoring eighth graders, but when she peered into the living room, she saw Carol-Ann sitting alone.

"Hi," Jeeter offered tentatively.

"Oh! *There* you are!" Carol-Ann said, standing up.

"Oh, boy," Jeeter muttered.

Carol-Ann strode over to her. "Now, look, Jeeter, I have to talk to you."

"Later?" Jeeter said, glancing toward the stairs.

"Now!" Carol-Ann said firmly. "Before four o'clock."

"That's what I was afraid of . . ."

"Jeeter Huff, do you remember what I asked you yesterday? Who gave you that headset in the first place?"

"You did . . ."

"That's right. And you notice I haven't asked you for it back."

"Thanks a lot," Jeeter said, making a face.

"So all I'm asking for is just one favor."

"Great," Jeeter moaned.

"One—sisterly—favor!" Carol-Ann repeated. "Now, is that too much to ask? From the person who gave you your magic thing in the first place?"

"But I don't know where it comes from—"

"Jeeter, don't change the subject!"

"All right," Jeeter sighed. "What is it?"

"I thought you'd never ask." Carol-Ann pulled out a long piece of paper from behind her back. "This," she said, waving it at Jeeter, "is a list of questions that I want you to ask the radio for me and my friends."

"Aw, Carol-Ann—"

"Do it, Jeeter. And I promise it's the only favor I'll ever ask you."

"Carol-Ann, this list is about a mile long!" Jeeter wailed.

"No, it isn't, don't exaggerate. It's just a few little questions—"

"There are a million questions here!"

"There are *not* a million questions! And all you have to do is read the list to the radio right before four o'clock, get the answers, give them to me and we're even."

Jeeter looked at the paper in her hand.

" 'Who does Robbie Goldstein really like?' " she

read. " 'Will Cindy get to go to the ninth-grade dance with David Wiggins?' Aw, come on, Carol-Ann, this is stupid. Don't make me—"

"I'll see you at five minutes after four," Carol-Ann said, heading for the kitchen. "I'm counting on you now, Jeeter . . ."

Jeeter made another face and looked at the list again.

" 'How much of North America will the social studies test cover?' " she read. "I can't ask Mason this stuff!"

Jeeter wiped her forehead. "How can I ask who Robbie Goldstein really likes!" She rolled her eyes. "Who *cares?*" Suddenly she frowned. "Hey, Carol-Ann?" she called toward the kitchen. "What do you mean, *'we're even'*?" But she didn't get an answer.

Slowly, she mounted the stairs to her room. "Read a list for Carol-Ann," she muttered to herself. "Boy!"

She walked inside and closed the door. It was getting close to "Mason time." Jeeter picked up the doll from her bed and held the list up in front of his eyes.

"Can you read this, Mason?" she asked. "Do you believe this list?" She sighed. The alarm clock next to her bed said 3:57.

"I just can't do it," Jeeter said softly to herself and the doll. "Carol-Ann shouldn't have asked me.

It's not fair. I never asked anything before. I bet it would all go away if I started now. I can't, I just can't." She took the headset from the doll and put it on. Maybe, she thought, Mason might tell me what to do . . .

She clicked the dial.

"Back in five," the DJ said.

". . . with the faves," Jeeter finished with him. "I can't even enjoy this now. If I escape again, Carol-Ann will only bother me tomorrow. She'll never let me alone . . ."

The little boy on the radio said: *"Jeeter, Carol-Ann is listening outside your door!"*

Jeeter's mouth dropped open, but the commercial with Mason and his mom went on without another word to her.

She took the headset off, inched quietly toward her door and yanked it open suddenly! Carol-Ann fell into the room, landing on the rug.

Jeeter said, "Hi."

"You rat, Jeeter," Carol-Ann said, quickly scrambling to her feet.

"Me!" Jeeter cried. "You were the one sneaking around up here, listening in and everything—"

"I just wanted to make sure you were doing what you promised."

"What I *what*?"

"—And I didn't hear you read the list. I didn't hear you ask a thing, Jeeter."

Jeeter looked down. She still had the list in her hand. She knew Mason wouldn't help her with this problem and she knew she couldn't ask him to. She pulled herself up as tall as she could and looked Carol-Ann in the face.

"I did," she said.

"You did what?"

"I have the answers you want."

Carol-Ann's whole face lit up. "You *do*? You really do? Oh, Jeeter, that's super! I'm sorry I yelled at you. Tell me what he said!"

"Stand over there," Jeeter commanded, pointing toward the door, and Carol-Ann obediently walked over. Jeeter went to her bed and sat down, scanning the list again quickly. Oh, boy, she said to herself again. She put the list on her lap and began to read.

" 'Who does Robbie Goldstein really like?' " she said out loud. She lifted her eyes quickly to watch her sister nervously chewing her lip and twisting her fingers. "Robbie Goldstein really likes Nancy MacBride," Jeeter said.

"Nancy Mac*Bride*?" Carol-Ann screamed and started to move toward Jeeter.

"Stay there!" Jeeter held up her hand, and Carol-Ann stopped. "Do you want these answers or not?"

"I do! But—*Nancy MacBride*? Jeeter, honestly, he didn't really say Nancy MacBride, did he? I mean, she's such a *wimp*! And Robbie never even looked at her before! I mean, she's president of the *Science Club*, Jeeter! She likes *bugs* and things!"

"Next question," Jeeter said. " 'Will Cindy get to go to the ninth-grade dance with David Wiggins?' Yes, she will, but only if she asks him herself."

"If *she* asks *him*? Are you crazy, Jeeter? Cindy would never do that! She can't ask anybody anything! She can't even ask to be excused to go to the bathroom, Jeeter!"

"Next question," Jeeter said. " 'How much of North America will the social studies test cover?' Canada."

"Canada?" Carol-Ann asked and stepped forward.

"Don't move," Jeeter said, and Carol-Ann drew back.

"Canada?" Carol-Ann repeated. "Only Canada? Nothing about the United States? Nothing at all? Nothing about Mexico? Nothing about—"

"Canada," Jeeter said firmly.

"Oh. Well . . . That's great! That's a lot less to study. What's next?"

Jeeter read: " 'What would impress Robbie Goldstein the most?' "

Carol-Ann made a face. "That was Lulu's question," she said quickly, "but I wanted to know, too.

Well . . . if the radio said he likes Nancy MacBride, it has to be because she's so scientific. I mean, Robbie Goldstein couldn't like Nancy MacBride for anything else, right? So I bet it's science that he likes. Bugs and things. Yech!" She sighed. "It must be bugs and things that would impress him the most. Okay, Jeeter, what's next?"

Jeeter read and answered the rest. The more she read and answered, the easier it became. Jeeter was having fun, making up answers to all of Carol-Ann's silly questions and watching Carol-Ann stand where she was told and listen. Several times, Jeeter almost laughed out loud, but she held it back.

That night, she could hear Carol-Ann on the downstairs telephone as she called all her friends. Holding Mason on her lap, Jeeter sat on the stairs with her hand over her mouth to stop her giggles.

"That's what I said, Lulu, *bugs*! . . . Well, how should *I* know what kind? *All* kinds! Spiders. Ants. Blecgh! I know it sounds awful! How about butterflies? Butterflies are pretty . . . *No*, I don't have a butterfly net!"

"*Yes*, Cindy, you have to ask him yourself. Well, gosh, Cindy, don't cry. These are modern times. Girls ask boys all the time. Just *do* it if you want to go with him . . . Yes, you can, Cindy . . . You *can* . . . Well, if you want me to, sure, I'll go with you, but I think it's silly . . ."

"That's right, Margie, only Canada. Don't even bother to study the United States, it's only *Canada* . . . Of *course* I promise!"

And on and on.

THIRTEEN

Safe!

By the next morning, Jeeter had almost put Carol-Ann and her questions out of her mind. All she hoped was that her sister would remember her promise and not ask her to talk to Mason ever again. She'd wanted answers, and Jeeter had given her answers, and now the whole thing had better be over.

At breakfast, she looked at Carol-Ann warily, wondering if her sister were cooking up something else for the radio, but Carol-Ann was singing happily to herself and paying no attention to Jeeter at all.

Big Beaver Elementary School was in the opposite

direction from Big Beaver Junior High, so Jeeter didn't have to walk even partway with her sister. She was happy to skip off down the street, dragging her book bag and trying to think of some new way to avoid Carol-Ann every weekday at four o'clock. She was thinking so hard she didn't hear Claudia come up behind her, and when Claudia cried, "Hi!" Jeeter jumped.

"Boy, Jeet, you didn't even have your headphones on and you still didn't hear me," Claudia said.

"Oh, I was just thinking," Jeeter said.

"You're always doing that," Claudia complained. "I don't do it enough and you do it too much."

They walked together in silence for a moment, and then Claudia said, "I'm so glad it's Friday! Aren't you? They should have Fridays every day!"

"But then you'd have no weekends," Jeeter told her.

"Oh. That's right. Well, then we could have a Friday . . . and then a Saturday-and-Sunday. And then another Friday, and then another Saturday-and-Sunday!" Claudia clapped her hands, pleased with her own idea.

Jeeter thought how much she looked forward to her weekdays now, but she didn't tell that to Claudia. Instead, she said, "Well, we wouldn't learn very much . . ."

"I don't seem to learn very much, anyway," Claudia sighed. "I wish I didn't have to listen and work. I wish it could all happen by magic."

"Things like that don't happen by magic," Jeeter said.

"Speaking of magic," Claudia said, "how are things going with your radio? You haven't said anything about it lately."

Oh, no, Jeeter thought. Now Claudia will ask me to do her schoolwork . . .

"It's fine," she answered in a small voice.

"You know . . ." Claudia began, "I finally told my dad about losing my locket. I mean, since I got it back, I didn't think he'd mind. And I just had to tell him how I got it back, Jeeter! The radio and everything!"

Jeeter said, "Uh-huh . . . And what did he say?"

"Well . . . I hope your feelings aren't hurt or anything . . . but he said you must have remembered seeing me drop it."

". . . Just like *my* father said," Jeeter sighed.

"He said the mind plays funny tricks. Sometimes you see things and you don't even remember seeing them. And then when you need to know them, they come back to you. He said hypnotists can make you do that."

Jeeter nodded slowly.

"Do you think that's what really happened, Jeeter?" Claudia asked.

They had reached the school and the bell was ringing.

"Come on," Jeeter called, breaking into a run. "We're late!"

Jeeter sat and stared at the blackboard while Mrs. Bonino wrote the math homework for the weekend on it.

No, she thought to herself. I didn't suddenly remember where Claudia dropped her locket. And I didn't make up Daddy's promotion. And I certainly didn't get out of the way of that bike by myself! I learned all of those things from the radio commercials—and Mason. And the boat ride, she thought—my fingers felt wet from that water! I'm sure it was real. But if Claudia doesn't believe me, I don't mind. No one has to believe me . . . It's all right. She bent over her notebook to copy the math.

As soon as Jeeter opened the door of her house that afternoon, she heard the sounds. Carol-Ann was crying. Loudly. Carol-Ann was screaming. No, she was sobbing. No, she was yelling. Jeeter stood still in the hall and listened. She could barely understand any words.

There was a pause in the tirade, and Jeeter could hear the calming voice of her mother. Her mother was home early—it was long before four. Jeeter frowned. What could be going on?

She made her way to the kitchen, where the sounds were coming from, and peeked in through the door. Carol-Ann was sitting at the kitchen table, her face buried in her arms. She was talking a blue streak, but Jeeter still couldn't understand anything. Mrs. Huff stood over Carol-Ann and was patting her shoulder, saying something soothing. Suddenly, Carol-Ann looked up and spotted Jeeter in the doorway.

"You!" she cried, getting to her feet and shrugging off her mother's hand. "You're gonna get it, Jeeter Huff!"

Jeeter cried, "Maa-aa," and began to back away. Suddenly there was a mad chase through the house: Jeeter, racing through the living room, through the family room, down the hall, up the stairs, down the stairs, into the kitchen, with Carol-Ann in full pursuit. At last, Jeeter ran to her mother, threw her arms around Mrs. Huff's waist and stood cowering behind her.

"Let me at her!" Carol-Ann was saying, trying to

grab at Jeeter, but their mother had had enough.

"Stop it, both of you!" Mrs. Huff yelled, and Carol-Ann stood, red-faced, near the table with her fists clenched. Jeeter still clung to her mother's back. "That chase was the most ridiculous thing you girls have ever pulled. Now, stop it, Carol-Ann. You will not touch your sister."

"I will. I'm going to turn her into cottage cheese!"

"No, you won't. Sit down."

Carol-Ann stuck her jaw out.

"I said sit down!"

Carol-Ann sat.

"Now, Jeeter, you go and sit down, too."

"At the same table?" Jeeter wailed.

"Sit!" her mother commanded.

Jeeter crept to the table, pulled out the farthest chair and sat.

"What did I do, anyway?" Jeeter asked. "I didn't even do anything . . ."

"You just ruined my whole life, that's all," Carol-Ann growled at her. "Only my entire life!"

"Carol-Ann, why don't you just tell Jeeter what it is that's bothering you," Mrs. Huff said, and leaned against the sink.

Carol-Ann pushed herself forward.

"But don't touch," her mother warned.

"I did everything you told me," Carol-Ann said

through her teeth to Jeeter. "Every single thing. And every single thing was *wrong*! Nobody will ever talk to me again! I don't have one friend left and I'll probably flunk out of school and it's all your fault, you and that s-stupid *radio*!"

"Carol-Ann, stop crying this minute," Mrs. Huff said. "That won't help anything. You life's not ruined and you won't flunk out of school. Just calm down and talk to your sister like a human being instead of a tornado."

Carol-Ann swiped at her eyes with a napkin. "Well," she said, pursing her lips, "you said Robbie Goldstein likes bugs!"

"No, I didn't," Jeeter said. "I said he likes Nancy MacBride. *You* said he likes bugs."

But Carol-Ann wasn't listening to Jeeter. "I went outside last night," she said, "and trapped a spider in a jar. It took me two hours! *Two hours!*"

"But I never—"

"I *hate* spiders!" Carol-Ann went on. "But I got one in a jar. To show to Robbie. And Lulu sneaked her brother's ant farm out of the house to bring to him. She did! An *ant farm*! She *wheeled* it all the way to school in her mother's *grocery cart* because she didn't want to even touch it! Even though it was all sealed in glass and everything!"

Jeeter said, "But I never—"

"And both of us showed those things to Robbie in study hall," Carol-Ann continued, "and what do you think he did?"

Jeeter said, "But I never—"

"He was practically *sick* right in front of us! That's what!" Carol-Ann finished. "He made noises like this: 'Blagh, ugh, yuck, gross!' and he turned *green* and he was *so* embarrassed because he was more afraid of the stupid bugs than *we* were!"

"But I never—"

"And now he won't talk to either one of us!"

"Aw, Carol-Ann," Jeeter said.

"And Cindy?" Carol-Ann wasn't finished. "Cindy asked David Wiggins to the ninth-grade dance. She could barely talk! It took her fifteen minutes just to get the words out. I was standing right there. And guess what David Wiggins said!"

"What?" Jeeter asked, wincing.

"He said he had to go visit his grandmother that night. He refused her invitation! Cindy was crushed beyond belief!"

"Aw, gee—" Jeeter said, near tears herself now.

"Of course, later on he came up to her and asked her to go the the carnival with him, so she felt a lot better."

"Oh, that's good!"

"Yes, that's good, Jeeter, but he isn't going to the

dance with her like you said he would! And that's not all!"

Jeeter said, "Oh, boy . . ."

"Our social studies test was about Florida! It was about California! It was about Arizona and New Mexico! It was about New England!"

Jeeter sighed.

"Do you know how many questions out of one hundred were about Canada? *Do you know how many?*"

"How many?" Jeeter asked weakly.

"*One!*" Carol-Ann yelled, rising from her chair.

"Don't touch!" Mrs. Huff cautioned.

Carol-Ann sat back down. "One," she repeated hoarsely. "And, oh, yes. Mary Lou."

"What about Mary Lou?" Jeeter asked. She couldn't remember the question about Mary Lou. Or the answer.

"Mary Lou was going to the beauty parlor with her mother last night, remember? She was thinking about getting her hair cut and she wanted your radio to tell her if she should?"

"Mary Lou . . ." Jeeter said. "She's the one with the ponytail down to her waist?"

"She *was* the one with the ponytail down to her waist. Your *radio* told her to cut it and get a frizzy permanent!"

"And did she?"

"Did she! She came to school with her head wrapped in a scarf! We got it off her in gym and you should see her! She looks like a dandelion!"

"Is it cute?" Jeeter asked faintly.

"It's *gross!*"

"It'll grow back," Jeeter offered, and thought to herself: I shouldn't have done that. I forgot which one Mary Lou was.

"You know what I think Jeeter?" Carol-Ann said, but she didn't wait for an answer. "I think that radio's a fake. I think you made everything up, and—"

"Now, just a minute, Carol-Ann," Mrs. Huff said. "Don't you go blaming Jeeter. You gave her that silly list, and no one forced you to look for bugs or not study or—or even cut hair! You were the ones who went blindly ahead with those plans and the only ones you should blame for their outcome are yourselves."

Jeeter squirmed in her seat. "I guess I'll go upstairs," she said.

"Jeeter, you stay right there," her mother said. "I don't want any more of this radio business."

"But, Mom—"

"No more, Jeeter! Imaginations are wonderful things—until they really get in the way! Do you understand me?"

"Yes," Jeeter said softly.

"Now you stay here in this kitchen. I want you to clean out the dishwasher from this morning and start mixing this casserole for supper. I've got some sheets to change, and Carol-Ann, you go right up to your room and study the work you should have studied last night!"

"But the test is over—"

"You can ask for a makeup. Now everyone—move!"

Everyone moved. Jeeter was alone in the kitchen. She began to take the dishes out of the dishwasher.

I'll miss today's message, she thought, looking at the clock. She stood on a chair to put away the plates and thought about Carol-Ann.

"I'll have to do something nice for Carol-Ann," Jeeter said to herself. "I had so much fun making up those answers—I guess I never thought she and her friends would really do the crazy stuff they did. . ." Jeeter smiled slightly. "I will do something nice to make it up."

Nodding her head, she climbed down from the chair. She put away the silverware and started to mix the ingredients for her mother's casserole.

She glanced at the clock. Nearly time, she thought. But I wouldn't make it now, even if I ran all the way upstairs . . .

At 4:10, Jeeter was finished. She covered the casserole and set it next to the stove. Then she went upstairs.

Mason was leaning against Jeeter's teddy bear, with the headset over his ears. Jeeter picked him up and looked into his face. His black pupils, surrounded by purple irises, stared blankly back at her.

"Hi, Mase," Jeeter said.

Mason stared.

"Carol-Ann won't be bothering us any more," she said. "That's what we wanted wasn't it?"

Mason stared.

"And I guess no one believes me any more, either," Jeeter went on. "Claudia's father told her my mind is playing tricks. Sometimes I start to wonder about it myself. And I was there!" She kissed Mason's bald head. "Funny, isn't it?" she asked.

Mason stared.

"And I missed today's message—if there was one—and tomorrow's the weekend, so there won't be anything for at least two days. I don't know, Mason—" Jeeter took a breath. "Was it you? Was it the radio? Or the headset sitting up there on top of your little round face? Or did I do it myself?"

She peered hard at the doll.

"You won't tell me, will you?" she asked with a little smile.

It took a split second if it took any time at all. Jeeter would never be sure. But she thought—

She thought she saw a pink eyelid close quickly over purple iris and black pupil.

Mason winked.